EMERALD PLANET

Laura Shenton

EMERALD PLANET

Laura Shenton

Iridescent Toad Publishing

Iridescent Toad Publishing.

Cover by Laércio Messias.

First edition. ISBN 978-1-913779-11-5

*Extra special thanks to Alathia Paris
for helping me bring this book to life.*

Chapter One

As the emergency room doors swung open, I felt the familiar rush of adrenaline coursing through me. Another patient, another life in my hands.

"He's got severe abdominal pain," the paramedic called out as they wheeled a stretcher past me.

Why had I taken this shift just to appease upper management? I needed to rethink how I gave back to the community.

I snapped on a fresh pair of gloves and followed to where the bed awaited the patient.

"On my count," I said, gripping one side of the backboard. "One, two, three..."

The patient groaned as we settled him.

"Let's get him to the operating room," I said.

"Inform whoever is on call for surgery."

As we rushed the patient towards the lift, I caught sight of the waiting room. It was packed to the brim, a sea of worried faces. I knew that for every patient we treated, three more would take their place.

Inside the lift, the doors slid shut, temporarily removing the scene from view. As we ascended towards the operating room, my mind raced with the countless tasks still awaiting me. There was no end in sight, no moment to catch my breath. This was the reality of emergency medicine – a constant, relentless battle against time and life's frailty.

I steeled myself for the long night ahead. The lift dinged, the doors opened, and I plunged back into the fray.

***

Three hours later, I emerged from the operating room. The patient had pulled through, but his journey was far from over. His survival now hinged on the long road of recovery ahead.

In the locker room, as I changed into my own clothes, the weight of my completed shift settled on my shoulders. The thought of a stiff drink to numb the edges of my exhaustion flitted through my mind.

"You ok, Doc?" a nurse asked, her concerned voice cutting through my reverie.

"Sure," I said, plastering on a reassuring smile. "I'm just tired."

The words felt rehearsed, a script I'd recited countless times before. I shrugged on my jacket, desperate to shed the mantle of responsibility, if only for a few hours.

The hospital's automatic doors parted with a soft hiss, and I stepped out into the night. I took a deep breath, relishing the cool, crisp air. Above me, a handful of stars pierced through the perpetual haze.

A sleek electric car idled at the curb – my pre-arranged ride. I raised a hand to catch the driver's attention, and then slid into the back seat.

"Where to?" the driver's voice crackled through the car's intercom.

I hesitated for a moment, then made my decision.

"The bar on Fifth Street."

I'd given him the address of the Rainbow Bar: a place most of my colleagues avoided like the plague, but for me, it was a sanctuary. Nestled in the heart of the city's interspecies district, it offered a slice of familiarity that I couldn't find anywhere else on Indikon. Looking forward to a drink, I leaned my head back against the soft seating and watched the cityscape blur past.

As we pulled up to the neon-lit entrance, I caught glimpses of the diverse clientele through the windows. Beings of all shapes and sizes milled about, their skin tones a vibrant palette that gave the bar its name. Purples, pinks, greens, and even a few plain-skinned individuals – humans like myself – mingled freely. To most plain-skinned humans, the colourful patrons were "aliens", but to me, they were a comforting reminder of diversity.

After thanking the driver and leaving the vehicle, I pushed through the door of the bar, immediately enveloped by the welcoming ambiance. The air was thick with the scent of exotic spices and liquors. A sign near the entrance spelled out the house rules in multiple languages: No fighting. No interplanetary politics. No offensive behaviour.

It was these simple guidelines that made the Rainbow Bar my refuge. Here, the pressures of my demanding job and the constant struggle to fit in melted away. I could simply exist, free from judgment or expectation.

I made my way to the bar, nodding at familiar faces as I passed. My usual seat awaited me, a worn leather stool that had possibly moulded itself to my form over countless visits. As I settled in, I couldn't help but reflect on my life. My demanding schedule left little room for meaningful relationships, and years of emotional guardedness made it difficult to truly connect with others. One-night stands had become my go-to solution – a way to release tension without risking my heart.

Lost in thought, I almost didn't notice the approaching figure. A woman with striking purple skin slid onto the stool next to mine, her iridescent eyes catching the low light of the bar. She smiled, revealing teeth that were just a shade too sharp to be human.

"Rough day?" she asked, her voice carrying a musical lilt that was common among her species.

I found myself smiling back, the stress of the day already beginning to lift.

"You could say that," I replied, signalling to the bartender for a drink. "But I have a feeling it's about to get better."

"I'm Lena," the purple-skinned woman said, her voice carrying a hint of amusement. "I'm an interplanetary trader."

My interest piqued. A trader: perfect. Someone accustomed to brief encounters, unlikely to seek anything long-term. I felt myself relax slightly.

"I'm Kate," I said. "I'm a surgeon at the hospital. Don't go doing yourself an injury – it's absolutely packed in there tonight."

Lena's laugh erupted, a melodious sound that rippled through the bar. Several patrons turned to look, their faces curious. The attention made me acutely aware of our connection, the spark of possibility hanging in the air between us.

Emboldened by the day's lingering adrenaline, I decided to dispense with the usual dance of small talk.

"Want to get out of here?" I asked, my voice low and tinged with invitation.

"Sure," Lena replied, an intrigued smirk playing at the corners of her mouth. "I was hoping you had something like this in mind."

She drained the last of her drink in one swift motion. I glanced down at my own untouched glass – my usual order, the bartender had placed it without me noticing.

Tonight, I craved a different kind of intoxication.

I quickly grabbed the bartender's attention and thrust a note at him.

"Keep the change," I said.

Lena's warm hand found mine, our fingers intertwining as she led me towards the exit. The short walk across the street to the hotel passed in a heady blend of anticipation and neon lights. As we approached her room, I felt a mixture of excitement and the faintest twinge of apprehension.

The door swung open, and I stepped inside, eager for what was to come. But instead of the expected passion, I was hit by a wall of stench – acrid, chemical, wrong. Before I could process the danger, a hand clamped over my mouth, armed with a cloth reeking of that same foul odour.

The room began to spin, colours blurring together like a kaleidoscope gone wrong. I tried to struggle, to cry out, but my limbs felt immobile. As consciousness began to slip away, my last coherent thought was a bitter realisation: I'd walked straight into a trap.

My eyes rolled back, and darkness claimed me.

Chapter Two

As my consciousness returned slowly, I struggled to open my eyes, each attempt feeling like an effort. Wondering what I'd had to drink last night, I raised a hand to my throbbing forehead, wincing at the sharp pain that lanced through my skull. The movement felt sluggish, clumsy.

"Is she awake?" a voice murmured from nearby, unfamiliar and tense.

Another voice, this one recognisable, responded:

"Now you have proof she's alive, I'll need my payment."

The memory of a purple-skinned woman smiling at me flashed through my mind, triggering a cascade of recollections.

My eyes snapped open wide, adrenaline finally cutting through the fog as I recalled the strange, acrid smell and the hand clamped over my mouth. I'd been drugged, abducted.

I blinked rapidly, taking in my surroundings. I was lying on a narrow bed in a small, dimly lit room. The walls were bare, utilitarian. No windows, just a single door.

A figure in a smart white lab coat stood by the door, his forest-green skin just about visible in the poor lighting. He held the door open briefly, allowing the purple-skinned woman to slip out quickly. He then shut it behind her with careful precision.

"Where am I?" I demanded, my voice hoarse and unfamiliar to my own ears as I tried to sit up, fighting against waves of dizziness.

The green-skinned man held out his hands in what I assumed was meant to be a calming gesture.

"No need for concern, Doctor Kate," he said, his voice low, almost soothing. "We don't mean you any harm."

Anger flared within me, cutting through the last of the chemical-induced haze.

"Then why am I here?" I demanded as I gestured around the unfamiliar room, my movements sharp and accusatory. "Wherever "here" is."

I glared at my captor, searching for answers. His stance was non-threatening, but the closed door and my pounding head told a different story. Whatever was going on, I was determined to get to the bottom of it – and find a way out.

"I understand your worries, Doctor Kate," the man said, his voice measured. "You are on the emerald planet known as Viridian."

My mind reeled. Viridian? That was light-years away from Indikon. How long had I been unconscious?

"What the..."

"Oh, my. Where are my manners?" he said, cutting me off and placing a hand on his chest in a gesture of contrition. "I'm Sebastian. It is my job to acquaint you with your position and help you with your transition."

He calmly took a few steps towards me, his posture relaxed as though we were having a casual conversation over coffee instead of... whatever this was.

"My transition?" I echoed.

The word sent a chill down my spine. Panic clawed at my throat as worst-case scenarios flashed through my mind. Organ harvesting? Slavery? Some bizarre alien experiment?

"You will be assisting A.I. robots where they are unable to operate, and training non-A.I. medics into the surgeons we need them to be," he replied with a reassuring smile that felt wildly out of place given the circumstances.

"No!" I shouted, my voice bouncing off the bare walls. "Take me back to Indikon."

Fuelled by fear and anger, I glanced around the room, torn between whether to scream for help or make a desperate attempt at escape. My overall disorientation made both options seem futile. I needed more information before I could act.

"I understand," Sebastian said, his expression thoughtful as he tilted his head slightly, studying me as if I were a particularly interesting specimen. "You're uncertain of your purpose here. Allow me to explain."

I tensed, ready to spring into action if necessary, even though a part of me knew I had no choice but to listen. Whatever was happening, whatever had brought me to this unfamiliar planet, the answers lay with Sebastian. So, with gritted teeth and clenched fists, I braced myself for what he was going to say next.

"We on Viridian have been at war with the Titians for years," he said, his expression sombre and his voice heavy with sadness. "In our efforts to minimise losses to life, we increasingly relied on technology."

I listened, still tense, but intrigued despite myself.

"While most A.I. robots are efficient and handle minor tasks well, our skilled surgeons and doctors grew older and passed away," Sebastian explained. "By the time we realised the need to train replacements, it was too late. We sought help from other planets, but were repeatedly refused."

The gravity of the situation began to dawn on me, but I remained silent, allowing him to continue.

"We have been watching you, our perfect candidate," Sebastian said, his voice taking on an urgent tone.

His words were deeply unsettling. How long had I been under surveillance?

"We need you to train our non-A.I. medics in the essential skills they desperately lack. They do their best to treat our sick and dying, but there's so much they need to learn. You must teach them," he insisted. "We promise to return you to Indikon once we have enough trained surgeons who are able to teach others."

"That's absurd," I objected, my medical training kicking in despite my indignation. "It takes years for someone to gain enough experience to operate safely. Besides, my patients back on Indikon need me."

Sebastian nodded, as if he'd anticipated my response.

"We understand your concerns, Doctor Kate. Your reputation is exemplary, which is why we chose you. You are renowned, but your absence from Indikon can be managed by others there. The fact that you have no immediate family or close ties also serves to make you the ideal candidate for this task."

The truth of his words stung more than I cared to admit.

"Great," I said, a bitter laugh escaping my lips. "Just because I don't have any commitments in my personal life, it doesn't mean that I'm fine with staying on a completely different planet against my will."

Sebastian visibly paled at my words, which served to remind me that despite his composed demeanour, he was as invested in this situation as I was.

A tense silence fell between us. I could see the desperation in Sebastian's eyes, the fate of Viridian resting on this bizarre plan. But I also felt the wrongness of my own situation – abducted, brought to a strange planet, expected to save a civilisation I knew nothing about.

As my predicament settled over me, I realised that my next words, my next actions, would shape not just my future, but potentially the future of an entire planet. The responsibility was overwhelming, but a small part of me – the part that had become a doctor in the first place – couldn't help but feel a twinge of curiosity and challenge.

Sebastian's demeanour shifted, his earlier politeness giving way to a cold, steely resolve.

"You will comply," he said, his voice now laced with an edge of threat. "There are no other options. We are at war and we must survive."

The sudden change in his tone was disturbing, but I gathered my courage, meeting his gaze defiantly.

"I refuse to comply," I said matter-of-factly.

As if on cue, the door opened immediately. Two more green-skinned men, both in dark clothing, entered the small room, their muscular forms dominating the space. They moved with practiced efficiency, closing in on me from both sides.

Adrenaline surged through my body. As they neared, in a feeble act of desperation, I thrust out my foot, aiming to kick the chin of the closest one, hoping to catch him off guard. My sluggish, drug-addled reflexes betrayed me.

With inhuman speed, he caught my foot mid-air, his grip firm but not painful. With almost gentle care, he lowered my leg back to the bed.

Before I could react, they moved in perfect synchronisation. Strong hands gripped my upper arms.

"No!!!" I wailed, my voice raw and desperate as panic overwhelmed me. "Someone help me!"

Even as the words left my mouth, I knew the futility of my cries.

"This won't do," Sebastian said softly, almost to himself, his expression a blend of regret and determination.

He gestured sharply to the two men.

"We'll have to advance this," he said firmly.

I saw a blur of movement in my peripheral vision. Before I could process what was happening, I felt rigid fingers pressing firmly against a point on my neck. A jolt of pain shot through me, followed immediately by a surge of nausea.

Consciousness slipped away for the second time, leaving me at the mercy of my captors and whatever plans they had for me on this war-torn planet.

Chapter Three

When consciousness returned, I found myself in a drastically different setting. Gone was the sparse room. Instead, I was slumped within the confines of a wire cage. My head throbbed, a reminder of my recent ordeals. As my vision cleared, I noticed a woman standing guard by the cage door, her posture rigid and alert.

Her legs were clad in opaque black tights, and she wore smart, functional black shoes. A simple pencil skirt, white blouse, and blazer accentuated her slender but womanly figure. The uniform's dark fabric contrasted sharply with her plain, pale skin, making her stand out even more against the drab surroundings. Her chestnut hair was tied up in a loose bun, revealing her soft features that seemed almost out of place against her stern demeanour.

I had no desire to speak to her. Instead, I took the opportunity to assess the room beyond the cage. Harsh artificial lights overhead cast a stark, cold glow that left no corner in shadow. There were no windows, no hint of the world outside. The walls, a dark and dreary charcoal grey, seemed to close in around the entire space, amplifying the room's oppressive air. At the far end of the room, an empty medical bed stood, its metal frame gleaming under the fluorescent lights.

Everything about this place was sterile and unwelcoming. Instinctively, I reached out towards the cage door, testing my boundaries. The guard shook her head slightly, a wordless warning. I frowned, my stubborn nature refusing to accept such a passive deterrent. Surely, I thought, there had to be a way out.

But then I heard it: a low, menacing buzz of electricity. The sound made me hesitate, urging caution where moments ago I'd been ready to act. An idea formed, born of desperation and a need to understand my predicament.

I slipped off my shoe. The guard watched,

curious but not intervening. I tossed the shoe towards the cage door, holding my breath.

The result was instantaneous and horrifying. Electricity arced through the air, latching onto my shoe with vicious intensity. I watched, heart pounding, as scorch marks bloomed across the leather. The unpleasant smell of burnt material filled the air.

A wave of nausea hit me as I realised how close I'd come to a terrible fate. With gratitude and resignation, I turned to the guard.

"Thanks," I mouthed silently.

She nodded, her expression unreadable.

The sound of footsteps caught my attention. Sebastian entered the room, his gaze fixed on me with an unsettling certainty. He tilted his head, studying me as if I were a particularly complex puzzle.

"When you're ready to begin teaching, we'll let you out of there," he instructed. "Until then, I can't trust you not to attempt escape. Alice will continue to guard you and provide anything you need for comfort. If you try to escape, the electricity will be lethal. Not the outcome I'd prefer, but it's your decision."

I wanted to argue, but thought better of it.

"I'll return in a few days," he said as he turned to leave. "Hopefully, you'll see the value in using your skills here."

I watched as he walked calmly away, a final mockery of my situation.

Once Sebastian had disappeared, Alice turned to look at me, her expression tinged with a sadness that caught me off guard.

"I understand that the thought of helping him, or us, is something you find abhorrent," she said softly, "but we truly need your assistance. It's not just about those who are dying now; it's about being able to save countless others later down the line. We've learnt our lesson."

Her head dropped, her words seeming to exhaust her. The silence that followed was heavy, filled with unspoken complexities.

I sank down lower onto the floor of my cage, my mind a whirlwind of conflicting emotions. Their desperation was palpable, their need genuine. But the methods they'd chosen, the violation of my freedom: it was unconscionable.

As I sat there, trapped in a cage on a war-torn planet, I found myself at an impossible crossroads. My ethical training as a doctor urged me to help those in need, but every fibre of my being desired to rebel against this forced servitude.

The buzzing of the electrified cage door served as a constant reminder of my predicament. I was here, whether I liked it or not.

Chapter Four

True to his word, Sebastian returned. By then, the monotony of confinement had begun to gnaw at my sanity. His arrival was almost a relief, a break in the endless cycle of discomfort and rumination.

"Have you changed your mind?" he asked, his gaze boring into me. "Will you help us?"

His intensity was almost unnerving, but still I met his stare with defiance.

"No," I said firmly. "I want to go home."

"I'm afraid that's impossible," he said, his expression hardening. "What happens next will be your fault."

The ominous words hung in the air as he swept out of the room, leaving me with a growing sense of dread.

"What do you mean?" I called out, leaning as close to the bars as I dared.

The urge to shake the cage, to physically express my frustration, was almost overwhelming. Suddenly though, the room erupted into activity. A stretcher burst through the door, wheeled in by four frantic orderlies. There was a man upon it, his green skin pale and mottled. Blood seeped from multiple wounds, staining the sheets crimson.

The four orderlies – a man and three women, evidently inexperienced – hovered around the stretcher, their movements panicked and unsure. They pressed bandages against the wounds, but it was clear they were out of their depth. The man's life was slipping away before my eyes.

Sebastian's voice crackled over a loudspeaker, filling the room with his ultimatum:

"You have a choice. Save this soldier's life, or watch the medics fail due to lack of training."

I glanced towards the door, where Alice stood like a sentinel. Her presence ensured there was no escape, no way to avoid this cruel test of ethics.

Minutes crawled by, each second marked by the soldier's laboured breathing and the medics' increasingly desperate efforts. I watched, my medical training screaming at me to intervene, while my pride and anger at my captivity held me back.

As the soldier's condition visibly worsened, I couldn't stand it any longer. The Hippocratic Oath I'd sworn years ago echoed in my mind, louder than my resentment.

"I'll do it," I shouted, my voice cracking with emotion. "Let me out."

The cage door opened with an anticlimactic hiss. Sebastian's voice returned:

"You can scrub-up at the wall before you join them."

I rushed to the small sink and began scrubbing my hands vigorously. It wasn't ideal, far from the operating rooms I was used to, but it would have to do. A life hung in the balance.

To my surprise, Alice appeared at my side, holding out a packaged surgical gown. As I moved to put it on, our eyes met. I saw relief and gratitude in her gaze.

"Thank you," I said, offering a small smile of acknowledgment before turning towards the patient, who was now on the room's only medical bed.

Approaching the wounded soldier, I felt a familiar calm settle over me. This was my element, where I could make a difference. Despite the circumstances, despite my anger at being manipulated, I knew I was doing the right thing.

"Alright," I said, my voice clear and authoritative, causing the medics to look at me, relief evident on their faces. "Let's help this man. And while we're at it, you're going to learn how to do this properly."

As I began to work, I pushed aside thoughts of my captivity and focused solely on the task at hand. I was a doctor first and foremost, and right now, that was what mattered most.

"Look for the smaller artery on the left side – pinch it," I instructed the nearest medic, acutely aware of the lack of proper equipment.

As the medic located and applied pressure to the bleeding artery, I quickly assessed our meagre supplies. With meticulous care, I began suturing to close each bleed. Gradually, the soldier's laboured breathing eased. Without monitoring machines, I relied on counting his breaths to ensure adequate oxygenation.

"You," I said as I pointed to a medic standing idle. "Start counting to monitor him."

Out of the corner of my eye, I noticed Alice standing silently to the side. She observed with a furrowed brow, her concern evident as time slipped away unnoticed amidst the demands of the procedure.

"Wash-up and then get him into a fresh gown," I told the medics. "You won't spot any problems if he's still covered in blood."

I followed my own advice, heading to the sink to clean myself. As the medics hurried to comply, the room slowly returned to its bleak, concrete state.

"I hate to ask," said Alice as she approached me hesitantly, "but could you please get back in the cage? I don't want to knock you out."

"Sure," I said with a sigh.

Compliance seemed preferable to nursing another headache. I scrambled back into the cage. The gate closed behind me, and I sank onto the floor, utterly exhausted.

"Alice," I called out, "he'll need someone to monitor him for a while. And antibiotics would improve his chances."

"Ok," she said. "I'll inform Sebastian. If you need anything else, write it down for me."

As she passed a pen and paper to me through the cage bars, I noticed there was no electrical hum surrounding me. Had the power been turned off?

It took me only five minutes to list the necessary surgical tools and supplies. Alice retrieved the list, her eyes scanning it quickly.

"Sebastian will see to it that you have everything you need," she said.

"Will he keep his word?" I asked, unable to

keep the scepticism from my voice. "If I train a new generation of surgeons, will he let me go home?"

Alice considered the question carefully.

"Yes," she said. "He will honour his promise. Every day, soldiers are dying out there; he's committed to resolving this quickly."

A sudden buzz signalled the electricity returning to the cage. Alice's expression turned apologetic.

"Get some rest," she advised.

Before I could say anything to her, Alice was already on her way out of the room. A new guard took her place, his demeanour stern and unyielding.

I sighed loudly, drawing the medics' attention, which I pointedly ignored. Figuring that I may as well rest, I lay back on the cot of my cage as they wheeled the patient out of the room. My mind raced with conflicting emotions – pride in having saved a life, anger at my captivity, and a growing realisation that I might be here for longer than I'd initially thought.

Chapter Five

A blaring alarm jolted me awake. Adrenaline surged through my body as I sat up, instantly alert. Alice burst into the room, pushing a stretcher along with four medics, this time three men and a woman, who moved with surprising efficiency.

My cage door hissed open, a silent command. I got out quickly, knowing resistance was futile. Another life hung in the balance, and despite my captivity, my medical instincts took over.

The new patient had multiple shrapnel wounds, presenting a complex challenge. I turned to one of the medics.

"What's your name?" I asked.

"Levon," he replied, already examining the patient with careful hands.

I checked the patient's pupils.

"I'm Sarah," said the young female medic, stepping forward to introduce herself. "He's injured in several places. How can you know which wound to treat first?"

I took a moment to look at Sarah, appreciating the earnest curiosity in her eyes. The situation was chaotic, and the air was thick with tension, but her question was a good one – direct and practical.

"In triage, our primary goal is to prioritise injuries based on the severity and the threat to the patient's life," I explained. "The first step is to quickly assess which wounds are most critical. See this deep laceration on his thigh? It's bleeding heavily, which means we need to control that haemorrhage immediately to prevent shock. However, this puncture wound near his lung is also serious. If his lung is compromised, he could have trouble breathing, which is equally life-threatening."

All four medics looked to me expectantly, eager for the next step.

"We have to make rapid decisions. Often, we'll address the most life-threatening issues first – airway, breathing, circulation. Once those are stabilised, we can move on to other injuries. It's about managing what's most urgent at the moment. Always remember, it's a balance between acting quickly and staying calm. Prioritise, stabilise, and then proceed methodically."

With Sarah's question answered and the initial triage done, I turned my full attention to the patient. The thigh wound was the most immediate threat, so I quickly applied a tourniquet above the injury to slow the bleeding. I motioned for Sarah to keep pressure on it while I prepared a suture kit. As I worked, I could feel the eyes of the medics on me. The room was tense, but there was no time for hesitation.

With the patient stabilised, I stepped back, taking a deep breath. I wiped my forehead with the back of my arm, feeling the adrenaline slowly ebb away. The medics were still standing there, watching intently.

"Good work, everyone," I said. "I didn't catch all of your names."

"I'm Jeremiah," one of the medics said.

"I'm Andrew," the last one replied, nodding respectfully.

"Sarah, Levon, Jeremiah, and Andrew," I confirmed, addressing them all.

***

As soon as I'd confirmed that the patient was going to be ok, the four medics took it upon themselves to leave the room, taking the patient with them, away to wherever it was they were headed. I could only assume that they were under orders.

"You were brilliant," Alice said quietly, her voice carrying a tone of genuine appreciation.

"Thank you," I said, feeling a wave of relief wash over me. "The medics did well too."

"I advise you to take a break while you've got the chance," said Alice, her smile kind as her gaze met mine.

I nodded appreciatively. There was nothing to be gained by rejecting the offer.

I followed Alice out of the room. We walked the sterile corridors until she stopped in front of a strictly functional-looking open-plan shower area. It was utilitarian to the extreme – no curtains, no partitions, just a plain shower head protruding from the tiled wall in an open space. I was beyond caring. I needed to wash away the grime that clung to me, to feel clean again, even if it meant sacrificing a bit of modesty.

"You can freshen-up here," she said reassuringly. "I'll bring you some clean clothes shortly."

Under the hot spray of the shower, I let the water wash away the tension. As I massaged shampoo into my hair, I couldn't shake the feeling of being watched. When I turned, Alice was there with a pile of clothes.

"Here you go," she said calmly. "I'll get some food sorted for you when we're back in the room."

As I rinsed my hair, I found myself puzzled by Alice's demeanour.

"Why are you being so kind to me?" I asked as I stepped away from the shower and began towelling myself. "Sebastian doesn't strike me as the type to prioritise my comfort."

Alice leaned against the wall, her expression thoughtful.

"He can be tough," she said. "Making all the hard decisions weighs on him. He chose me to guard you because he knew I'd make sure you had what you need to do his bidding and feel more settled here."

I pulled on the clean clothes, considering her words.

"Well, thank him – not for the abduction, obviously, but for having you here to make things smoother."

"He'll appreciate that. Just keep doing well, and eventually, he may let me get you out of here."

"Oh," I replied, unable to hide my scepticism.

Chapter Six

In what I assumed was several days later, within the gruelling routine of mending broken bodies one after the other, the minimal operating room had become my classroom, each patient a new lesson in survival against the odds.

I had since worked with more groups of medics. I had to start from scratch every time, teaching the basics all over again. It was exhausting, but there were certain satisfactions in watching their skills improve, however incrementally.

Alice had proven to be an invaluable ally. When I suggested turning off the alarm to make the environment less hostile for everyone, she made it happen without question. Now, as the light flashed its silent alert, I sat up in my cage, waiting for the familiar opening of the door to signal that I was needed once again.

I exited my cage, and Alice stood there, surgical gown in hand. She'd become attuned to my methods, anticipating my needs with an efficiency that bordered on telepathy. I slipped into the gown, grateful for her quiet support in this challenging environment.

This time, the stretcher bore the first female patient I'd seen since my abduction. Her green flesh was torn and blackened, her shoulder a mess of charred tissue. The damage spoke of some kind of pulse weapon, far beyond anything I'd seen back on Indikon.

Having placed the patient on the bed, the medics moved instinctively to stem the bleeding.

"Don't!" I shouted across the room before lowering my voice to explain. "She's been burned. We have to work differently on her. Bandages will stick to the burns."

I snapped some gloves on and moved closer to the medics as they watched me with wide-eyed expectation.

"Once the main damage has been repaired, the two biggest concerns will be infection and replacing the skin," I said, turning to Alice as a new worry crossed my mind. "Do you have donors we can use for a skin graft after she's recovered enough for one?"

"Good question," Alice replied. "I shall have to ask Sebastian. It's unlikely, given the situation."

I nodded, pushing down my frustration. I couldn't let it hinder my work.

I turned back to the patient, my mind already racing with potential solutions. The wounds were more extensive than I'd initially thought, requiring every ounce of my concentration and skill.

As I worked, I found myself marvelling at the physiology beneath my hands. Despite the obvious differences – the green skin, the slightly different organ placement – there was a familiarity that was almost comforting. Life, it seemed, followed certain patterns regardless of planet.

The medics watched as I navigated the complex web of damaged tissue, explaining each step as I went. Their eagerness to learn was exemplary, a reminder of my own early days in medicine. Despite the circumstances, I felt a spark of pride in passing on my knowledge.

Time proceeded in a haze as we fought to save the woman. My back ached, my eyes strained in the harsh light, but I pushed through. This was what I was trained for, what I lived for. The fact that I was doing it on a different planet, under duress, seemed almost irrelevant in the face of the immediate need to heal.

As I finally stepped back, exhausted but satisfied that we'd done all we could, I caught Alice's eye. She nodded, understanding without words that I needed a moment to collect myself.

I stripped off my gloves and gown, heading to the small sink to get clean. How long had I been here now? The lines between captive and surgeon, teacher and prisoner, were blurring in ways I never could have anticipated.

Chapter Seven

I exhaled a deep breath as the medics removed yet another patient from the room. My head throbbed, a dull ache born of exhaustion and poor nutrition. My muscles felt fatigued, and my back was in pain. The torrent of countless surgeries and lack of sleep bore down on me, threatening to crush my spirit. Before I could voice my discomfort, Alice appeared beside me, her movements purposeful.

"We've got some hot food for you," she said softly, gesturing to the small table at the far side of the room. "Things aren't going well at one of our battles. You'll need your strength to keep going."

As I slumped into the chair, Sebastian strode into the room, his presence filling the space with an air of authority. He took a seat across from me, his piercing gaze commanding my engagement.

"So, how do you think things are going?" he asked, his casual tone striking a discordant note in the tense atmosphere.

I could no longer conceal my frustration and resentment.

"How are things going?" I said bitterly, furious at the nonchalance of his approach. "Seriously? Horrible lighting, no fresh air for I don't know how long, rotating medics – I can't even remember their names. I haven't had a decent sleep since I got here."

"All good points," Sebastian began, "but..."

I stood abruptly, causing the chair to scrape loudly against the floor behind me.

"No, not points: reality," I said angrily, refusing to be patronised. "I'm one surgeon. I simply can't operate on every patient on this planet. There is physically no way for me to take care of all of them. It's not possible."

As quickly as it had come, the fire drained out

of me. Suddenly, nothing seemed important. The food before me looked bland and unappealing. The dark walls of the room seemed to close in from every angle.

"Very well," Sebastian said, turning to Alice in the hope that she would know what to do.

Alice's response was crisp and professional, but her words barely registered. My mind had entered a foggy, detached state. I was vaguely aware of Sebastian giving more instructions, but they seemed to come from a great distance.

"Take her to her room," I heard him say. "Make sure she gets some rest before you bring her back."

"Come on," Alice urged gently as she slid her arm around my waist, supporting me in my state of exhaustion.

My body responded automatically, but inside, I felt hollow. It wasn't until a warm, pleasant light hit my face that I realised we were outside. The shock of fresh air and open space jolted me back to awareness.

Before me stretched an urban landscape, but unlike the congested cities of Indikon, this was more spacious. Wide, empty streets sprawled out like arteries, their surfaces shimmering slightly under the sun's rays. As I took a step forward, the ground beneath me felt strange, a blend of unfamiliar materials forming a smooth, resilient surface. I glanced around, expecting to see crowds, but there was hardly anyone there. Birds – or at least creatures that seemed like them – chirped from the tops of trees that lined the walkways. Their melodies were both alien and familiar, a comforting reminder that some things remained universally constant.

"Better?" Alice asked kindly, smiling as she watched my expression with knowing eyes.

I nodded mutely, still taking in the unfamiliar landscape. My body, starved of natural light, began to absorb the vital element it had been missing for weeks, a palpable sign of my system desperately trying to make up for what it had lost. The fog in my mind began to clear; replacing it was the dawning realisation of how close I'd come to a complete breakdown. The windowless confines of the makeshift operating room had taken a toll I hadn't fully comprehended until this moment.

As warmth and vitality seeped back into my body, I turned to Alice.

"Thank you," I said, my voice thick with emotion.

The depth of my gratitude went beyond words. She had quite possibly saved my life with this simple act of kindness.

Standing there under the glorious sky, I felt a complex mixture of emotions wash over me: relief at feeling more like myself again, anger at the circumstances that had brought me here, and a grudging admiration for Alice's perceptiveness and care.

"It's beautiful, isn't it?" she said, her voice carrying a hint of melancholy. "But don't be fooled. This place is an exception, not the rule. Our building is in a secret location in the middle of nowhere, far removed from the battlegrounds and unknown to the enemy. The vast majority of Viridian looks nothing like this. The beauty you see here is carefully maintained, a sanctuary amidst the turmoil."

I looked back at the serene landscape, the tranquillity now tinged with a sense of fragility.

"The medics have been transporting the most complex cases here. For every patient you've helped them save, there are many more out on the battlegrounds that won't make it."

Alice's words hit me hard, a stark reminder of the reality that lay beyond this quiet enclave. My mind swirled as I imagined the battlegrounds, the suffering and chaos. I closed my eyes, trying to stave off the rising tide of panic.

"I know you didn't ask for any of this," Alice said gently, sensing my distress. "Take a moment to breathe. Just be. Your wellbeing is just as important as anything else."

My head was full of conflicting thoughts. Exhausted, I clung to the fresh air, the sunlight, and the simple act of being present, drawing my strength from Alice's small but vital act of kindness.

Chapter Eight

As consciousness gently pulled me from the depths of sleep, I realised with a start that I was no longer in the cage that I had grown strangely used to. Instead, something wonderfully soft enveloped me. I rolled onto my back, my fingers instinctively exploring the texture of the duvet draped over me.

A bed. A glorious, luxurious bed. For a moment, I allowed myself to revel in the simple pleasure of comfort, something I hadn't experienced in what felt like years.

As tempting as it was to linger in this pleasant cocoon, my bladder had other ideas. When I sat up and swung my legs over the side of the bed, my feet found slippers placed with uncanny precision, as if someone had anticipated exactly where I'd need them.

With that small act of consideration, reality came crashing back. Alice. Sebastian. My abduction. The joy I'd momentarily felt at my improved surroundings evaporated as I remembered the true nature of my situation: I had a nicer place to sleep, but I was still very much a prisoner.

I surveyed the room, noting three doors. The first revealed a closet filled with basic clothing and scrubs. They served as a stark reminder of my purpose here – saving lives at the cost of my own freedom.

The second door led to a bathroom that would have been the envy of my younger self. All those years of saving and scrimping during my residency flashed through my mind. What good had it done me? Here I was, alone on a foreign planet, surrounded by luxuries I'd once only dreamed of. A bitter laugh escaped me as I wondered if living a little more in the moment might have somehow prevented this situation.

After taking care of pressing needs, I splashed water on my face and studied my reflection. To my surprise, the woman staring back at me didn't look as haggard as I'd been expecting. It was a small mercy, but one I clung to.

"Hey, I thought I heard you stirring around in here."

Alice's voice startled me, even though I recognised it right away. I turned around to see her standing in the doorway.

"I'm up," I replied, my stomach rumbling loudly. "How long was I asleep?"

"Two days," she answered, concern evident in her tone. "I was starting to worry that you were going to need medical care."

"Wow!" I said, surprised. "I knew I was tired, but still…"

As I moved past Alice towards the closet, her natural scent wafted over me. An unexpected heat crept into my cheeks as thoughts I hadn't dared entertain suddenly surfaced. Flustered, I tried to cover my reaction.

"I've managed to convince Sebastian that you need good food and fresh air. I'm going to take care of both before you dive back into the fray," said Alice, her eyes following me as I changed clothes. "Sebastian is still under the impression you should be able to work as the A.I. robots do."

I couldn't help but chuckle with cynicism as I pulled on a pair of trousers.

"I know he seems demanding," said Alice, "but his heart is in the right place. He doesn't want to lose more people, which is why he wants to make your life here on Viridian more comfortable. We appreciate that being cooped up in here can't be good for your wellbeing, so it has been decided that you can go out and work in one of the hospitals nearby. You'll train the medics there for two months before they are sent out into the field."

"Two months?!" I exclaimed, the implications hitting me hard. "That's barely enough time to make sure they can do basic procedures, much less emergency surgery!"

"We don't have much of a choice," said Alice. "If you don't train them, we have no hope at all. The bottom line is that we need you to do what you can; it's the only way to give our people a fighting chance. The A.I. robots just aren't capable of doing more than the basics. When something goes wrong, they can't see where the problem is to fix it."

I exhaled deeply, becoming acutely aware of the immense responsibility that remained squarely on me.

"Food first, save the planet later," I said, attempting to lighten the mood.

"You forgot fresh air," Alice reminded me with a smile that stirred something deep within me.

Even in captivity, I found myself wondering if I might be capable of falling in love after all. I quickly shook my head, trying to dispel such dangerous thoughts. Stockholm syndrome was real, and I couldn't afford to fall victim to it, no matter how genuine Alice's kindness seemed.

"You're right," I agreed, forcing myself to focus on the present. "Fresh air is just the thing."

As we prepared to leave the room, I couldn't

help but feel a mixture of emotions: gratitude for the improved conditions, anxiety about the challenges ahead, and a confusing attraction to Alice that I knew I shouldn't indulge. Whatever lay ahead, I knew I had to honour my primary goal – helping as many medics and patients as possible while holding on to the hope of regaining my freedom.

Chapter Nine

I hadn't seen a single glimpse of my surroundings on the way to the hospital facility. The vehicle that had brought me here had windows tinted so darkly that no light or view had penetrated its interior, reminding me that I was still very much a prisoner.

When I got out of the vehicle, it was a relief to see Alice waiting for me outside the hospital. With no time to lose, she quickly led me through the labyrinth of sterile corridors and bustling activity. Its sheer scale was overwhelming – without her guidance, I might have wandered aimlessly for hours.

As we approached what I assumed were the operating rooms, I noticed a group of fifteen medics lining the hallway. Their eager faces betrayed a blend of excitement and apprehension. I took a deep breath, steeling myself for what needed to be said. Public speaking had never been my forte, but I needed everyone to understand the gravity of what lay ahead.

"Listen carefully," I began, my voice echoing slightly in the hallway. "There are many of you here for training – training that should take years. Yet circumstances demand you learn it in mere months because lives hang in the balance."

I glanced at Alice, who offered an encouraging nod. Drawing strength from her silent support, I continued.

"Prepare for gruelling hours split between patient care, surgeries, and intensive study. Sarah, Jeremiah, Levon: you'll be team leaders. Choose your groups of five. Remember, you're accountable for their mistakes. Your prior experience with me means higher expectations."

I scanned the faces of everyone present for any hints of doubt.

"Has anyone got any questions? No? Alright

then. Let's begin," I said, my mind already racing ahead as I turned to address Alice. "How many patients have we currently got?"

Before she could answer, alarm lights began to flicker ominously throughout the corridor. My body tensed, instinctively preparing for action.

"Where's the receiving area?" I asked, already reaching for a clean gown from a nearby cart.

"Levon," said Alice. "Escort Doctor Kate to the ambulance bay. Take your team with you. The rest of you: focus on your assigned tasks until further notice."

I had to sprint to keep up with Levon as he led the way. At the same time, I tried to catalogue details of our route. If I ever hoped to escape, knowing the layout would be crucial. For now though, the patients mattered more. Besides, there were probably security measures in place, but that was a concern for another time.

As we burst through the doors to the ambulance bay, I saw three emergency vehicles backing up, lights flashing urgently.

"How do we alert the other teams?" I asked, my mind already triaging potential scenarios.

Andrew, one of Levon's medics, stepped forward confidently. He strode to a wall-mounted phone and spoke clearly:

"Doctor Kate says we need all three teams here, stat."

I nodded approvingly. Initiative like that would be invaluable in the coming months.

There was no time to dwell. As patients on stretchers began pouring in, I threw myself into the controlled chaos of triage. Levon's team, newly dubbed 'Group L', sprang into action, whisking the most critical cases towards the operating room.

Sarah's group was next. I was struck by her composure. There was a practiced efficiency to her movements that went beyond what I'd taught. I filed that observation away for later – she would be an asset in a crisis.

Just as I was considering how to navigate back to the operating room, another ambulance arrived. It was fortunate I'd waited – Jeremiah's inexperience might have cost a life otherwise.

Back in the operating room, the scene that unfolded was gruesome. A patient with a horrifically mangled knee was rushed in, followed by a medic clutching the detached limb. Blood still seeped from the ragged wound where veins and arteries had been violently severed.

"Tighten that tourniquet!" I commanded, my mind already mapping out the complex procedure ahead. "Jeremiah, order more blood – he's lost a dangerous amount already."

This was beyond the medics' current abilities. I'd have to take the lead.

"Alright, people," I said. "We're racing against time to save this leg. Move!"

In crisis mode, issuing orders came as naturally as breathing. I made a mental note to channel this confidence outside the operating room – it might prove useful in navigating this strange new world I found myself in.

"Observe closely, everyone," I said. "This is valuable experience for future emergencies."

The familiar rhythm of surgery took over. My hands moved with precision as I began to clean the catastrophic wound. Even as muscle memory guided my actions, I forced myself to narrate each step.

"Watch the major blood vessels carefully," I instructed. "We'll unclamp each one only after ensuring a proper connection to its counterpart in the severed limb."

Time seemed to blur as I worked, my voice providing a constant stream of explanation. Jeremiah proved to be a capable assistant, anticipating my needs with growing confidence.

Periodically, Alice would appear at the observation window, her presence a silent reminder of the larger stakes at play. In my commitment to getting the patient stable, my world narrowed to the intricate dance of scalpel, suture, and skill.

Hours later, as I guided Jeremiah through the final sutures, exhaustion began to creep in.

"Keep the stitches even," I reminded him. "A clean line will promote better healing."

As I stepped back, peeling off my gloves, Alice appeared beside me, her expression unreadable.

"I'm needed elsewhere, aren't I?" I asked, already anticipating the answer.

"Actually," she replied, surprising me, "the others seem to have managed. But your expertise in reviewing their work would be invaluable."

As we moved to check on the other patients, my mind churned with questions. For now though, I had a job to do. These medics needed guidance, and despite the circumstances, I found myself invested in their progress.

I allowed myself a moment of pride for what we'd accomplished today. Lives had been saved, skills honed. It wasn't freedom, but it was something. And in this strange situation, I'd take whatever small victories I could find.

Chapter Ten

Days blurred into weeks, weeks into months, until time lost all meaning. My life on Viridian had settled into a routine, punctuated by the daily walks between my allocated apartment and the hospital, which, as it turned out, was a considerable distance away from the battlefields, which I had yet to see. As the season shifted, I found myself donning a coat to ward off the encroaching chill. The winter here was mild compared to what I'd known on Indikon – whether due to Viridian's climate or my specific location, I couldn't be sure.

The first hints of holiday celebrations began to appear in the shops lining my usual route. Unfamiliar decorations and festive goods filled the window displays, hinting at traditions I had yet to understand. In what felt like a calculated show of trust, I was permitted to venture out alone, most likely being watched from somewhere.

I treasured these rare moments of pseudo-freedom, savouring the illusion of normalcy as I explored the local eateries. The vendors had come to recognise me, efficiently scanning my food card without a word. I assumed Sebastian, or whoever truly pulled the strings, settled the accounts. The intricacies of Viridian economics were beyond my realm of concern – or so I told myself.

Adapting to the local cuisine had been a challenge. Where my home planet favoured plant-based diets, Viridian meals were decidedly carnivorous. The shift in nutrition had reshaped my body in surprising ways. I'd gained weight, yes, but it manifested as dense muscle rather than excess fat.

As I collected my order from a street vendor, the disposable container warm in my hands, I settled at a nearby table. Even in Alice's absence, I could almost hear her voice, providing commentary on our surroundings. The area was clearly Viridian's equivalent of an upscale shopping district. Immaculate pavements hosted leisurely shoppers, the atmosphere one of casual affluence.

The normalcy was disorientating. If not for the constant awareness of my captivity and the certainty that any attempt to flee would be met with swift consequences, I could almost believe I was back on Indikon, albeit in an unfamiliar city.

This thought sparked a sudden curiosity. How representative was this polished area of Viridian as a whole? With nearly an hour before Alice was due to meet me, an idea took root. Risky, perhaps, but the desire to see beyond my carefully curated environment was overwhelming. If caught, I would have to think up an excuse later.

I hailed one of the autonomous vehicles that served as public transportation. As I slid into the seat, I addressed the A.I. driver.

"I'd like a tour beyond the city, please. Show me everything – from the wealthiest districts to the poorest."

The A.I. driver took his time, probably working to process my unusual request.

"Right you are," he said.

As we pulled away from the pristine streets I knew, the reason for the city's carefully maintained façade became painfully clear.

Beyond the city, Viridian bore the scars of conflict. Entire blocks lay in ruins, evidence of bombing campaigns that could have happened years ago or more recently. The contrast was stark and unsettling.

I hadn't witnessed any explosions during my time here, but the steady stream of casualties flowing into our hospital spoke volumes. It seemed Viridian was a planet struggling to maintain appearances while grappling with dwindling resources and ongoing hostility.

The further we ventured from the city, the worse the conditions became. Mountains of rubble and refuse choked the streets. Among the detritus, I spotted children playing, their faces streaked with grime but their laughter undimmed by their surroundings. It was a poignant reminder of resilience.

A lump formed in my throat as I absorbed the reality of life beyond my carefully controlled bubble.

"I've seen enough," I said softly, tapping the seat to get the driver's attention. "Take me back, please."

***

As the vehicle neared the city, the meal I'd eaten earlier sat heavily in my stomach, at odds with the gnawing hunger that I now imagined plagued most of Viridian's population. The realisation was a bitter pill to swallow – while I enjoyed regular access to running water and abundant food, countless others struggled for basic necessities.

My mind drifted to my home planet, where nobody had to go without a basic level of comfort; everyone had a place to live, with access to good nutrition and healthcare. Here on Viridian, the disparity was profound.

Although I yearned to confront Alice about the circumstances on Viridian, a nagging voice warned me against bringing attention to my unauthorised excursion. Still, Alice had become more than just my guard – she was my confidante, perhaps even my closest friend. The thought both comforted and unsettled me.

As the vehicle pulled up to my original departure point, I scanned my payment card, hoping that whoever dealt with the mechanics of it wouldn't look too closely at each transaction.

"Thank you," I said to the A.I. driver, genuinely grateful for the eye-opening tour.

"I'm not sure what you were expecting to see," he replied. "The land beyond the city hasn't changed in years. The city's alright due to all the money that's been invested in it – a desperate effort to maintain morale for the fortunate minority, if you ask me."

His candour surprised me. It struck me that it would be a lost opportunity not to take advantage of it.

"I'm not from your planet," I admitted. "I'd really like to understand how things work here."

"It wouldn't make sense to you," said the driver, his tone suddenly cold and dismissive. "Forget I said anything."

His terse response was a clear indication of

the climate of fear and secrecy permeating Viridian society.

Once out of the vehicle, as I stood on the pavement debating my next move, I spotted Alice approaching. Without thinking, I rushed towards her, engulfing her in a spontaneous embrace. Embarrassed by my outburst, I anxiously stepped back with an awkward laugh.

"I'm sorry," I said quickly.

"No, you're fine," Alice reassured me, her eyes scanning our surroundings warily. "What brought that on?"

Sighing deeply, I led her to a nearby bench.

"I know I wasn't supposed to," I said as we sat down, "but I got one of the A.I. drivers to take me on a tour beyond the city. Alice, it's awful out there. We live in this bubble of luxury while others have nothing."

Alice's expression fell, resignation and understanding crossing her features.

"Kate, you're brilliant. I should have known

you wouldn't just accept my vague explanations about Viridian," she said cautiously, choosing her words carefully. "We've been at war, in one form or another, since before my grandparents were born. Many have tried to fix this mess, but it has been going on for so long now that it seems impossible."

"It feels so long ago that Sebastian had me brought here," I admitted. "Back then, I had no idea how bad the situation was. This whole thing is more severe than I could have imagined."

As a deep sadness settled over me, I couldn't help but think of home. Had I not been abducted, I could have been living a normal life, blissfully unaware of Viridian and its troubles.

"I know that deep down, you're still upset about what Sebastian did," Alice said perceptively. "It's easy to judge him, but he was truly out of options. There was no alternative."

"There's always an alternative," I countered, my voice firm.

With a heavy sigh, Alice stood up.

"Walk with me," she said. "I'll try to explain our history. But remember, we must keep our voices low."

It upset me to think that Alice was under duress. She was too good for this awful situation. A wild idea grabbed me.

"Alice," I whispered urgently, "why don't we just leave? My planet would grant you asylum. You could escape all of this."

The pained expression that crossed her face told me everything.

"Kate, I do like you, but..."

"But?" I prompted, already bracing myself for the rejection.

"You're my assignment," she said softly. "I can't get involved beyond friendship. It's a line I can't cross."

"He's never going to let me go, is he?"

Alice couldn't answer the question. The realisation crystallised in that moment: if I wanted freedom, I would have to seize it myself.

Pushing aside my emotions, I refocused on the more pressing issues at hand.

"How can we help those beyond the city?" I asked. "They are clearly in need. There must be something we can do."

"The best thing we can do is ensure the soldiers survive and win the war," Alice offered, her response measured. "If the other side takes control, things could get much worse. They'd enslave us all."

"Aren't you already enslaved?" I countered, struggling to stay quiet as my frustration boiled over. "You have no freedom. If I could just show you how things are meant to be, you'd understand what you're missing."

"If we all left, who would remain to make the necessary changes?" Alice challenged.

It was clear to me that Alice saw something here worth fighting for, something worth saving – even amidst the devastation and despair. It was hard for me to grasp fully, coming from a place where such turmoil was unimaginable, but I couldn't ignore the strength of her conviction.

Chapter Eleven

The conversation with Alice haunted me for days, her words intertwining with the unpleasant truth of Viridian's reality. The disconnect between the polished façade of the city and the war-torn outskirts gnawed at my conscience.

I found myself grappling with questions that seemed to have no clear answers. What had driven Viridian into such a prolonged, destructive conflict? How had diplomacy failed so spectacularly that entire communities lay in ruins? My home planet had known war centuries ago, and occasional skirmishes still erupted, but nothing approaching the scale of devastation I'd glimpsed here.

Troubled by the enormity of the situation, yet acutely aware of my limitations as an outsider, I channelled my energy into the one area where I could make a tangible difference: training new surgeons. The task took on a new, almost sacred significance. Every surgical technique I demonstrated, each diagnostic skill I honed in my students, carried the weight of countless future lives saved. I began to see each lesson as a small act of rebellion against the senseless violence plaguing this planet.

On the surface, Alice and I slipped back into our easy friendship, but an undercurrent of tension remained. My longing for home, once a dull ache, now burned with renewed intensity. I knew that if an opportunity for escape presented itself, I would seize it without hesitation.

As the weeks passed, my teams grew more confident and capable. They handled increasingly complex cases with minimal supervision, their skills blossoming under the pressure of real-world application. It wasn't until Sebastian's unexpected visit that I fully grasped how far they'd come.

His imposing figure cast a shadow over my lunch table in the hospital cafeteria.

"Doctor Kate," he began, his tone uncharacteristically hesitant, "do you believe the majority of hospital staff are now ready to operate independently?"

I chewed thoughtfully, considering my words.

"They could," I said. "Most have taken my instruction and adapted it creatively to address unforeseen complications. Are they reflective of practitioners who have had the benefit of years of experience? No. But they're far more capable than when we started."

Sebastian rubbed his chin, his expression unreadable.

"I think it's time to deploy them to the battlegrounds," he declared. "Having them work on-site in the medical tents could save crucial time and lives."

Horror washed over me at the thought of what it would be like for the newly-trained surgeons to work in a war zone. It was one thing to perform surgery in a controlled environment, but to operate under fire would require a completely different mindset.

"We need them, Doctor Kate," Sebastian pressed, a note of desperation creeping into his voice. "Think of how many additional lives could be saved with more immediate treatment."

I shook my head, overwhelmed by the implications. Sebastian sighed heavily and took a seat across from me, his usual air of authority momentarily replaced by something almost vulnerable.

"Look, I know it's far from ideal," he conceded. "That's why I want you to accompany them, at least initially. You can assess the conditions first-hand and make any necessary adjustments to their approach."

He moved to reach for my hand, but I instinctively pulled back. If he noticed my recoil, he didn't show it. I tried to keep my expression neutral, but inside, a storm of fear and apprehension brewed. This was uncharted territory for me – nothing in my training or experience had prepared me for the sheer chaos of a war zone.

"Once they're established," he continued, "you can return here and begin training the next cohort. We've postponed this for as long as possible, but the need is too great. With stronger medical staff out in the field, we can address critical injuries without delay."

I wanted to protest, to tell Sebastian that I wasn't ready for this. But the words caught in my throat, unable to form. My mouth opened, but no sound came out.

"Alice will ensure you're packed and ready to go first thing tomorrow morning."

With those ominous words hanging in the air, he abruptly stood and strode away, leaving me alone with my churning thoughts.

As the reality of the situation sank in, a spark of hope ignited within me. This could be my chance – my only chance – to escape. Surely a battlefield would have some form of space transport. If I could just get my hands on a ship...

I knew that deserting Viridian would be an act of profound cowardice. People were depending on me. But then, I imagined myself back on Indikon, in the safety of my home, far removed from the horrors and hardships. The comfort and familiarity of a normal life beckoned to me like a siren's call. I could almost feel the peace of a life untouched by war. The pull of this fantasy was strong, and I hated myself for entertaining it, but I'd had my fill of being put in awful situations against my will.

***

Alice was already packing when I burst into my apartment, slightly out of breath. One look at her face told me she sensed something was wrong.

"We need to talk," I said.

Understanding flashed in her eyes, tinged with a sadness that caught me off guard.

"Let me finish getting this ready for you," she said softly.

As we packed, I discreetly added items I hoped would aid my escape: a flashlight, rope covertly taken from a supply closet, sturdy running shoes. Alice watched me with a mixture of resignation and something that looked almost like pride.

Her hands moved with practiced efficiency, but as the bag began to fill, her movements became more erratic. With her back to me, she fumbled with a shirt. I noticed her shoulders trembling. My heart sank, but I stayed quiet, unsure of what to say.

Suddenly, she stopped and turned to face me, tears welling in her eyes.

"This is hard for me," she said, her voice cracking with emotion.

"Is it the fact that I want to go home? Or..." I hesitated, searching her eyes, "that there might have been something more between us, if circumstances were different?"

"All of that," Alice admitted, "and the fact that I'll be sent to the front lines – not to oversee you, but for combat duty."

Her words hit like a physical blow. Outrage coursed through my veins as I began to pace, my mind racing. The injustice of it all threatened to overwhelm my every thought.

Alice placed a gentle hand on my arm, halting my frantic movements.

"I'll be ok," she said, uncertainty in her voice. "It's meant to be a promotion, actually."

It disgusted me that the powers that be had the audacity to class whatever this was as a promotion. As I tried to tame my anger, I suddenly found myself looking at Alice with a different intensity. Her display of raw emotion had stirred something deep within me. I saw a reflection of my own longing in her eyes – a vulnerability and unspoken feelings. Time seemed to come to a stop as we stood there, connected by a bond that went beyond our roles and the chaos around us.

"I can't imagine not having you in my life," I confessed. "You've been more than just a friend – you've been my anchor. I think... I think I've fallen in love with you."

Alice froze, her eyes widening in shock. For a moment, a strange silence hung heavily between us, the air thick with uncertainty. Then, slowly, a soft smile tugged at the corners of her lips as a blush crept into her cheeks.

"I... I didn't expect this," she murmured, her voice barely above a whisper as she looked down, her fingers fidgeting nervously with the hem of her blazer. "But... I feel the same way."

"You do?"

"Yes," she admitted, gaining confidence. "I've tried to hide it, but... I've fallen for you too... But listen: you deserve a better life. It's not fair of Viridian to keep asking so much of you, to keep using your skills to fix our problems. You didn't cause this conflict; you shouldn't have to sacrifice your future for it."

"If I could find a way for you to come to Indikon with me, would you?" I asked desperately, already sensing her answer.

The pain in Alice's expression told me everything. Understanding and sorrow mingled within me.

"It's ok," I assured her, fighting back tears of my own. "I don't blame you. Viridian is in your heart. It's your home."

"I want you to know," Alice said sadly, "that meeting you has changed me. Regardless of what happens tomorrow, I'll carry a part of you with me always."

I nodded, unable to speak past the lump in my throat. In that moment, I understood that our connection, though born of unpleasant circumstances, had irrevocably altered both our lives.

Chapter Twelve

The world was still shrouded in darkness when Alice slipped from the bed I'd shared with her, the whisper of her movements barely audible as she headed for the shower. I fumbled in the gloom, my fingers searching for any evidence of our night together – discarded clothing, a forgotten item that might betray us. I couldn't assume the apartment wouldn't be checked once I'd gone. I couldn't bear the thought of Alice being in trouble because of me.

As I moved about, my mind replayed the events of the night. It had been nothing short of transformative. By candlelight, we had explored each other with a reverence bordering on worship, our hands and lips mapping uncharted territories until exhaustion finally claimed us. Falling asleep in Alice's arms, I had experienced a sense of belonging I'd never known before.

The bitter irony of the situation wasn't lost on me. After years of searching, I had finally found someone who made me feel complete. And now, I was due to leave her behind with little hope of ever returning.

I should have been focusing on preparing myself mentally for the challenges ahead, but all I could think about was Alice, the warmth of her body still lingering beside me. As I lay there, thoughts of the impending departure settled heavily on my chest. I wanted to reach out, to hold on to this fleeting moment of peace and love, but I knew I couldn't. Each minute that passed was a painful reminder of the inevitable separation.

Alice emerged from the shower, her presence a bittersweet comfort. I forced a smile as she approached, her eyes searching mine for reassurance.

"I'll be ok," I whispered, though the words felt hollow even to my own ears.

"I'd better head off as soon as I'm dressed," Alice said sadly. "The longer we spend saying goodbye, the worse it will be. Besides, if anyone asks, I didn't sleep here."

"I understand," I said solemnly.

Alice dressed hurriedly, the urgency palpable in her movements. With her chestnut hair still dripping wet and darkened from the water, she came over to my side of the bed. Standing over me, she bent forward and hugged me tightly. The touch of our embrace conveyed more than any words could.

"Stay there," she said softly. "Let's not make this any harder than it needs to be."

The lump in my throat prevented me from speaking. I watched in silence as Alice turned and left the apartment, leaving behind an echo of her presence that remained long after she was gone.

I glanced at the clock and realised time was slipping away. Thankful for the distraction, I pushed aside my swirling emotions and focused on getting ready to leave. Alice's departure still hung heavy in the air, but I couldn't afford to dwell on it now. Sebastian would be waiting for me outside.

***

All thoughts of escape and home evaporated the moment I stepped into the medical tent. The residue of war assaulted my senses, the acrid smell of burning and antiseptic mingling in the stuffy space filled with makeshift operating tables.

"How close are we to the front?" I asked one of the soldiers nearby.

"About two kilometres, give or take," he said, his expression grim. "The chance of a stray bullet reaching us is minimal. We're just about managing to hold ground, but if things intensify when the enemy next attacks, we'll relocate to maintain a safe distance."

"I understand," I replied, uncomfortable with the unpleasant reality.

"Your team will be here soon," he explained. "All incoming wounded will be triaged here first. Once they're stabilised, we'll transport them back to the main hospital for recovery and continued care."

I fought to keep my expression neutral, suppressing a grimace at the abysmal working conditions.

"What about the medical staff who've been manning this post? Where are they?" I asked, searching for any sign of experienced personnel.

"There weren't any. Just the A.I. robots. They did what they could to stem blood loss until patients could be evacuated to you."

"Seriously?!" I replied, disbelief washing over me.

The soldier shrugged, unable to conceal his embarrassment.

Shaking off my shock, I snapped into action.

"Right," I said. "First priority: have the A.I. robots begin sanitising the operating tables. We can't risk infection with open wounds in these conditions."

Chapter Thirteen

The days blurred together in a frantic whirlwind of treating wounded soldiers and weathering enemy attacks. The air was thick with the scent of smoke and burning debris, a constant reminder of the conflict raging just beyond our frail perimeter. Even in the quieter moments between gunfire, tension hung in the air like a storm waiting to break. Countless times, the distant rumble of artillery echoed all around, each explosion reverberating in my chest. The ground seemed to constantly tremble in sympathy, as if the earth itself had grown weary of the violence.

Finally, during some long-awaited downtime, as I passed the makeshift restrooms, my exhausted gaze fell upon an unexpected sight: a small shuttlecraft, sitting unattended and inviting. In that moment, a reckless plan crystallised in my mind. Without allowing myself time to second-guess or falter, I approached the craft, opened the door, and clambered inside.

The interior was reassuringly familiar, not too dissimilar to the shuttles back home. My hands, moving almost of their own accord, found the start button. As I eased the control stick forward, instead of the expected horizontal motion, the craft began to rise.

Panic flared as I realised the differences between this shuttle and anything I'd operated before. I desperately scanned the console for a way to ascend. Spotting a promising-looking button, I jabbed at it. To my immense relief, the shuttle responded, climbing rapidly into the cloud cover.

Hovering momentarily in the misty sanctuary, I searched the panel for a way to input co-ordinates. My fingers then danced across the screen, programming the route to my home planet. Just as I finished verifying the course to Indikon, a voice crackled over the radio:

"Shuttle three-fifty-eight, come in, please. What are you doing?"

"Going home," I muttered to myself, a mixture of determination and defiance colouring my tone.

The radio squawked again, more insistent this time:

"Shuttle three-fifty-eight, you are not cleared to leave the planet."

The response switch was tantalisingly close. Without hesitation, I flicked it on.

"Bite me," I said mutinously.

"Excuse me?" said the voice on the other end, sounding genuinely shocked. "I think we have a communication problem. I thought for sure that you said 'Bite me.'"

"Roger that," I confirmed, a grim smile on my lips. "That's exactly what I said. Bite me. I'm going home."

With that, I switched off the radio, silencing any further attempts to dissuade me.

The shuttle surged forward as it breached the atmosphere. In a disorientating blur of motion, I found myself on the other side. The vast expanse of space unfurled before me, a tapestry of stars and distant planets.

An automated voice, stilted and artificial, broke the silence:

"It will take twelve hours and twenty-three minutes to reach your destination."

"Got it," I mumbled, my earlier bravado giving way to bone-deep weariness.

As the adrenaline of my impromptu escape began to ebb, exhaustion crashed over me in waves. I fervently hoped the shuttle's autopilot was reliable – to stay conscious for the entire journey felt impossible. As the stars streaked by outside, I allowed my heavy eyelids to close, surrendering to the pull of slumber.

***

It felt as though I'd only just closed my eyes when a jarring alarm shattered the silence of my cocoon inside the small shuttle. The automated voice, now urgent and loud, cut through the cacophony:

"You are about to enter the atmosphere of Indikon."

As I quickly studied the console buttons again, another voice crackled through the speakers, human this time:

"Shuttle three-fifty-eight, please identify yourself. We have no scheduled arrivals today."

Tears welled in my eyes. The familiar cadence of my home planet's dialect – a subtle difference I'd almost forgotten – hit me like a physical blow. It was a bittersweet reminder of all I'd left behind, and all I was desperately trying to reclaim. Swallowing hard, I pressed the response switch.

"Indikon Tower Control, this is Doctor Kate Bennett. I was taken by the Viridians and managed to escape. Permission to land?"

After a pause that felt eternal, the reply came:

"Permission granted. You will be met by

security. You are required to provide a statement."

Despite my relief at being so close to Indikon soil, my stomach churned with a feeling of unease.

Chapter Fourteen

As the shuttle began its descent, the autopilot handled the landing with surprising gentleness. The craft settled onto the ground with barely a bump, causing me to release a breath I hadn't realised I'd been holding. The moment the door hissed open, several members of the security force rushed towards me.

"If you'll follow me, Doctor," one of them said curtly.

Rising after hours of confinement, my body protested vehemently. Every muscle screamed in agony, but the officers' impatient postures made it clear that rest wasn't an option. Grimacing, I climbed out of the shuttle and forced myself to walk, with two officers in front of me and another two behind.

What came next was far more gruelling than I could have imagined. The ordeal of being abducted and forced to teach surgery under duress paled in comparison to the battery of tests, examinations, and interrogations. First came the medical exam, invasive and thorough. Then, a decontamination cycle that left my skin raw and tingling. Hours dragged by, punctuated by increasingly pointed questions and suspicious glances. Finally, they provided me with a clean set of clothes that felt alien against my skin. I quickly dressed and was then ushered into a small, sterile room furnished only with a basic table and two chairs.

Exhaustion and frustration finally overwhelmed me.

"Am I in trouble?" I demanded, unable to keep the edge from my voice as I sat forward in my chair. "Is there any chance I can go home and continue this tomorrow?"

A stern-faced man with striking blue-toned skin, who had introduced himself as Calvin, fixed me with an unyielding stare from across the table.

"No," he said matter-of-factly. "We must verify your story and understand why you didn't attempt to return home earlier."

"Seriously?!" I said indignantly. "I've no idea how long I've been away; I was forcibly taken from Indikon and made to work on Viridian. What more verification do you need?"

"I can't let you back onto the planet without following the security procedural process to the letter," he said coldly. "This isn't about doubting your story or your identity. We have strict regulations in place for a reason. It's for your safety as much as it is for everyone else's. Skipping any steps could compromise security, and I can't make exceptions."

His words were measured, almost rehearsed. It was clear that no amount of pleading would change his mind; Calvin was clearly a man of rules, and those rules were his shield.

A groan escaped me as I massaged my temples, trying to stave off the migraine I could feel building. The lack of sleep and the stress of my escape were finally catching up with me, fraying the edges of my composure.

"How can I make you understand?" I pleaded, desperation creeping into my voice.

"For now, we'll finish taking your statement. Then you'll be placed in a hotel for a few days while we investigate. We need to rule out every possibility."

"Look," I said, "put as many guards as you need outside my hotel door. I've got nothing to hide. All I want right now is to eat and sleep."

Calvin nodded, a flicker of sympathy crossing his features. As if on cue, the door opened, and he glanced at the newcomer before turning back to me.

"Stay here," he instructed, rising to his feet.

Left alone once more, I found myself fighting a losing battle against exhaustion. As the minutes ticked by, my eyelids grew heavier, my head drooping despite my best efforts. In the end, sleep claimed me, dragging me down into a fitful slumber filled with dreams of home and exile, and of a journey that, despite my return, felt far from over.

Chapter Fifteen

I jolted awake, my heart racing. A noise had startled me from my uncomfortable slumber, and as consciousness flooded back, so did the reality of my situation. The sterile room around me felt like a cage, a stark reminder that I was back on Indikon but far from free.

I let out a groan of disbelief.

"Seriously," I shouted, my voice hoarse from sleep and frustration, "is someone going to let me out of here, or do I have to burn the place down?"

As if summoned by my outburst, Calvin appeared in the doorway, his blue-tinted face a mask of forced calm.

"I need you to simmer down," he said bluntly.

His words were like fuel to a fire. I let out a laugh that bordered on hysteria.

"Simmer down?!" I answered back. "Have you been abducted before and made to feel like you're the one who did something wrong?!"

I stood, my body protesting after hours of stillness.

"You're free to go," said Calvin, his words stopping me cold.

"What?" I uttered, my anger replaced with suspicion as I searched his face for any sign of deception.

"You've passed all the checks. You're free to go."

Calvin led me through the facility, his boots echoing in the sterile corridor. The silence between us was awkward, a stark contrast to the constant barrage of questions I had endured during the security checks. I tried to find something to say, but I had nothing. He seemed just as uncomfortable, his eyes darting around as if searching for an escape from the tension.

We walked past rows of nondescript doors and blinking security panels, the lighting harsh and unpleasant. My heart pounded louder with each step, anticipation and unease swirling within me.

"I'll hand you over to Paige," Calvin said. "She'll escort you back to your apartment."

"Is that really necessary?" I asked. "I can find my way on my own."

"It's not for security reasons, if that's what you're worried about," he said, offering a small, almost apologetic smile as he shook his head. "The authorities just want to offer you a bit of courtesy. You've been through a lot, and they think you deserve some extra care."

It was nice to finally be believed.

"Paige will be here soon," he said as he gestured towards the exit. "I'll leave you to get some fresh air."

The moment I crossed the threshold, I was overwhelmed by a flood of emotions. The sky stretched out above me, an endless expanse of blue that seemed almost surreal after the confinement of the facility and the war-torn battlegrounds of Viridian. The air was warm and filled with the scent of blooming flowers and fresh earth, so different from the bleak environments I had just left.

Ahead of me, the urban landscape was a harmonious blend of nature and modernity. Towering buildings with sleek, reflective surfaces reached up towards the sky, catching the sunlight and scattering it in dazzling patterns. Between the structures, trees lined the pathways, their leaves rustling slightly in the gentle breeze, providing shade and a splash of green amidst the concrete.

The beauty of Indikon was genuine. Unlike the city in Viridian, it wasn't a façade designed to compensate for the scars of conflict that lay beyond.

"Hey," a voice said.

I turned to see a woman in a suit, similar to the one Alice wore.

"I'm Paige," she said. "I'll be escorting you to your apartment."

As Paige drove us through the strangely familiar city, a complex mix of emotions washed over me: relief at being back, certainly, but also a weird sense of disconnection. Everything was as I remembered, yet I felt like a stranger in my own world.

"Your job is there for you when you wish to return to it," Paige said gently, cutting through my reverie. "The powers that be assume you'll want to recover from your ordeal. Either way, you may resume working whenever you feel ready."

As we pulled up outside my apartment building, the reality of my situation began to sink in. I was back, but everything had changed – including me. I felt a pang of something unpleasant, unsure as to whether it was nostalgia or regret. I found myself wondering what Alice would say. I had to forcibly push the thought away.

As Paige handed me a new set of keys and some sandwiches, the freedom I'd longed for now felt oddly hollow.

Alone in my apartment, I felt adrift. The urge

to do something childish – like jump on the bed – warred with lethargy. As I ate, my mind kept drifting back to Viridian, to Alice, to the life I'd left behind.

Chapter Sixteen

The sun was just peeking over the horizon as I stepped out of my apartment building. The city was already bustling, the streets busy with pedestrians going about their morning routines. As I walked, I couldn't help but marvel at the towering skyscrapers and gleaming infrastructure – sights I'd once taken for granted that now seemed almost ostentatious.

As I approached the hospital, a feeling of déjà vu washed over me. With its blue-tinted glass, the sleek architecture stood unchanged, a testament to the consistency of life here on Indikon. It was as if my captivity on Viridian had never happened, the world here continuing its steady march forward without missing a beat.

Taking a deep breath, I entered the building. The scene that greeted me was both achingly familiar and strangely alien. The emergency room pulsed with a rhythm I once knew by heart – a symphony of efficiency and purpose. Nurses glided between beds with practiced ease, holographic displays flickered with patient vitals, and the soft hum of advanced medical equipment filled the air.

As I observed the seamless operation around me, I was struck by a bittersweet realisation: this was luxury. Here, skilled assistants anticipated every need, allowing surgeons to work their life-saving magic unencumbered. The contrast with my experiences on Viridian was jarring. There, I'd juggled countless roles – co-ordinator, instructor, surgeon, and more – often working with limited resources and under immense pressure.

I felt guilty as I watched a team efficiently treat the victim of a hover-car accident. The advanced care the patient received was remarkable, yet I couldn't help but think of the Viridians struggling for basic medical attention amidst the perils of war.

I continued my walk through the familiar corridors, struck by how easily I blended in.

Whether it was my lingering air of belonging or simply the busy nature of the hospital, no one questioned my presence. The anonymity felt both comforting and unsettling.

Pausing at the observation window of an operating room, I watched as a surgical team came towards the end of a routine procedure. The precision and abundance of resources at their disposal were a far cry from the makeshift operating theatres I'd left behind.

"May I help you?" someone behind me asked, interrupting my reverie.

I turned to see a vaguely familiar face – a doctor I'd trained with years ago, though his name escaped me.

"Doctor Kate," he said, recognition gleaming in his eyes. "It's good to see you back."

"Um, hi," I managed.

"It's a while since I've seen you around here."

"It's a long story," I said, too drained to expand on the details. "I've been doing some work on another planet. They've been at war for years and have a chronic shortage of medical staff – especially surgeons."

"That sounds incredibly challenging," he said, his voice tinged with empathy. "I can't imagine how hard it must be to work under those conditions."

"Every day was a struggle," I said, my voice steadying as I recounted the hardships. "The hospitals are overwhelmed, supplies are scarce. It was heartbreaking to see so much suffering."

"I wonder if there's anything Indikon could do to help," he mused aloud, his tone thoughtful yet resolute.

"We could send some of our surgeons there," I said, half jokingly.

"Hey, that's not a bad idea."

I hadn't been expecting him to say that.

"Really?" I asked, not quite daring to believe what I'd just heard.

"Yes," he answered. "If you need a few volunteers, I might have some people who would be up for that. I'm sure they would value the experience and appreciate the opportunity to help out. Just leave your number with my secretary, and I'll have them call you."

As I pondered the possibility of organising an aid mission to Viridian, doubts gnawed at me. Would it even be diplomatically feasible to gather a team of surgeons for such a perilous endeavour? Viridian's history of being refused help from other planets added another layer of complexity. Had they already asked Indikon for help and been declined?

Still, I had to hold on to hope.

"Thanks," I said, grateful that my colleague, whose name I still couldn't remember, had so readily offered such a simple solution. "Let's swap contact details. I'll call you once I've got everything sorted."

One way or another, I had to make this work. When it came to dealing with Viridian, it would have to be on my own terms. If I was going to help them, it would be as a free person, armed with the resources, people, and determination to make a real difference.

Chapter Seventeen

The next couple of weeks passed in a whirlwind of activity. I threw myself into assembling a team of volunteers, each chosen for their skills and their willingness to venture into the unknown. The enormity of our mission hung heavy in the air during every meeting, every preparation.

It was during this time that I encountered unexpected support from the authorities of Indikon, which came as a welcome surprise. It was an acknowledgment, a tacit admission of their failure to protect me from the abduction I had endured. Whether out of embarrassment or concern for repercussions, the authorities were eager to support me, not just as an individual but as a leader of a crucial mission to aid Viridian.

As our departure day approached, I found myself feeling hardly any remorse about leaving Indikon. Instead, a sense of purpose filled me, driving away any lingering doubts. Viridian was where I needed to be, where I could make a real difference.

Our transport ship was a far cry from the tiny shuttle I'd stolen for my escape. This vessel was enormous, its hold packed with medical supplies, food, and clean water – the building blocks of hope for a battered planet. As I settled into my seat for the journey, I couldn't help but reflect on the irony: I was now more determined than ever to return to the very planet that I had once yearned to escape.

As we neared Viridian airspace, the radio suddenly crackled to life, startling us all.

"This is Viridian Air Control," a commanding voice sliced through the static. "Please identify yourself."

Bracing myself, I gripped the transmitter tightly in my hands.

"Viridian Air Control, this is Doctor Kate Bennett from Indikon," I announced, my voice steady despite the tension coursing through me. "We're here on a humanitarian mission, bringing essential supplies and medical aid."

After a tense pause, the voice on the other end responded:

"Access denied."

Something inside me hardened. Alice was so close now, and I wasn't about to let bureaucracy stand in my way.

"Listen to me," I said, my voice carrying an extent of confidence I didn't know I possessed. "If Viridian still needs medical assistance during this time of war, you will permit us to land. I have something that will be extremely beneficial to your cause."

There was another tense silence, broken only by muffled voices in the background. Finally, the radio crackled back to life:

"You are cleared to land in Section C. Only Doctor Kate Bennett will be allowed to leave the ship. Doctor Bennett, you will be escorted into the building to meet with Sebastian. Do you understand?"

"Yes, perfectly. Thank you," I said, a blend of relief and apprehension coursing through me as I prepared for landing.

As soon as I left the ship, I was escorted by stern-faced guards to a clinical-looking facility that loomed ominously in the distance. When I stepped inside, the sterile walls and cold lighting only added to the sense of unease.

I was promptly marched into a stark room, where my eyes locked onto a familiar figure: Sebastian. He stood rigidly, clad in a crisp white lab coat that contrasted sharply with his dark expression. His glare bore into me with unmistakable displeasure, making it clear that my presence was neither expected nor welcomed.

"You!" he said with a bitter snarl. "How dare you show your face here?"

"Sebastian, I..."

"You abandoned us. You ran like a coward."

The accusation stung, but I refused to let it show.

"I escaped because..."

"Because what?" Sebastian interrupted, his voice dripping with venom. "Because you couldn't handle the pressure? Because our suffering was too much for your delicate sensibilities?"

"I escaped because I was a prisoner," I said, fighting to keep my voice steady.

Memories of fear and captivity came flooding back, but I steeled myself, swallowing the rising tide of emotions. I knew I needed to tread carefully, to win him over somehow.

"Give me one good reason why I should give you the time of day," he said, an infuriated smirk playing on his lips. "What do you want?"

"I've got something for you," I countered, making sure to meet his gaze as I held on to the fact that I had done so much for Viridian already. "I'm here to help. I'm here to offer Viridian aid in its time of need."

I noticed a shift in his expression, his features relaxing ever so slightly.

"Ok," he said, a deep sigh escaping his lips as he took a seat and gestured for me to do the same. "I'm listening."

"Thank you," I said, settling onto a hard chair and preparing to make my case. "I've brought a team with me from Indikon. I've got skilled surgeons ready to hit the ground running. We've got medical supplies – everything from basic first aid to advanced surgical equipment. There's enough to last for several months, and plans for sustainable aid beyond that. But, Sebastian, I have conditions."

"Let's hear them," he said warily.

"My team and I will maintain full autonomy over how we function. No coercion: we're here because we want to be."

Sebastian was now looking at me with something that resembled respect. I knew this was the perfect opportunity to push for more.

"Alice is to be part of the project," I said bluntly. "Her skills, her dedication: they're essential to making this work. She was an asset to me when I was last here, and I require her assistance this time around."

Silence stretched between us, taut as a wire. Sebastian's brow furrowed in deep contemplation, betraying an inner conflict. It was clear that my proposal had struck a chord, stirring emotions and considerations he hadn't anticipated.

Finally, he spoke, his voice low and strained.

"You drive a hard bargain... Doctor."

I allowed myself a small smile. Now the real work was about to begin.

Chapter Eighteen

Standing in the drab, generically functional government office, my heart pounded as I waited. My thoughts were consumed by Alice. I desperately wanted to see her, to know she was alright. I hoped she wasn't angry at me for having left; the last thing I'd wanted was to cause her pain. Gripped by the anxiety of the moment, I clung to the hope that she would understand, that she would still care for me.

Finally, after what felt like an eternity of tension, the door creaked open, and there she was, looking well and as beautiful as ever. Her eyes widened in shock, and her mouth fell open as she registered my presence.

"What are you doing back?!" she exclaimed, her voice a mixture of disbelief and something else I couldn't quite place.

I took a step forward, fighting the urge to rush to her, to close the gap between us that had felt like an insurmountable chasm for so long.

"Alice," I said, her name a prayer on my lips. "I've come back: to help, to make things right... and for you."

"But you escaped," she said, confusion etched across her features. "You were free. Why would you want to sacrifice that?"

I swallowed hard, gathering my courage.

"I couldn't stop thinking about Viridian," I said. "I couldn't stop thinking about *you*."

"I don't understand," she whispered.

"I've persuaded the powers that be," I said, my voice growing stronger as I took another step forward. "You're to be my assistant. I've brought a team of volunteers with me from Indikon. We'll work together, side by side, just like before. Only this time, I'm here through choice."

Her breath caught in a small gasp that sent ripples through me.

"Alice, being away... it taught me something – something I should have realised long ago. I can't live without you. Every day I was gone, every moment I was supposedly free, I felt more trapped than I ever did here."

Alice's hand trembled as she reached out, her fingers barely grazing my arm, as if attempting to check whether I was real.

"You came back... for me?"

I nodded, feeling tears prick at the corners of my eyes.

"For you, for Viridian, for all of it. I realised that my place is here, helping those who need it most. And my heart... my heart is wherever you are, Alice."

The silence that followed was electric, charged with desire and longing. Then, slowly, a smile broke across Alice's face.

"I thought I'd never see you again," she admitted, her voice thick with emotion. "I've missed you so much."

"I'm here now," I assured, taking her hand in

mine and revelling in the warmth of her touch. "And I'm not going anywhere."

As we stood there, I felt a sense of rightness settle over me. The challenges ahead were daunting – a planet at war, countless lives hanging in the balance. But I knew, with a certainty that ran to my core, that this was where I belonged.

"We have a lot of work ahead of us," I said, giving Alice's hand a gentle squeeze. "The casualties of this war need our help, and I intend to do everything in my power to save as many lives as we can. It won't be easy, but with you by my side, I know we can make a difference."

"Together," Alice agreed, determination hardening her gaze.

I felt a surge of hope. The road ahead would be fraught with challenges and heartache, but worthwhile. In Viridian, I had found my purpose. More than that, I had found my home – not in a place, but in a person: in Alice's unwavering strength, in her compassion, in the love that had drawn me back across the stars.

Epilogue

In a blur of exhaustion and determination, everyone worked tirelessly to aid the people of Viridian. The mission was gruelling, but we pressed on, driven by the hope that our efforts would make a difference.

Several years later, it wasn't just our medical aid that assisted Viridian; it was Indikon's diplomatic influence that brought about peace. Indikon's leaders managed to negotiate a settlement between Viridian and Titiana, ending the war that had ravaged both planets.

With the war finally over, Viridian began to rebuild. The scars of conflict were everywhere – damaged buildings, shattered lives, and the lingering pain of loss. Despite the devastation, there was resilience, a determination to rise from the ashes and create something new. Slowly but surely, the places torn apart by war were restored, even though many would bear the marks of suffering for a long time to come.

Through it all, Alice stood by my side. We faced unimaginable challenges together, and in the process, our love sustained us. As Viridian recovered, so did we, building a life together on the planet we had fought so hard to save.

While I had initially come to Viridian through no choice of my own, and had spent much of that time yearning to leave, the unexpected twist of fate turned out to be worth it in the end. Viridian had become a place of peace and healing, where I found both purpose and love. Out of the darkest times had emerged a beacon of hope.

9 781913 779115